THE EAST PUDDING CHRONICLES
Plight of the Witch Watchers

To Billie,
Merry
Christmas !
CR.Berry
X

The East Pudding Chronicles

PLIGHT OF THE WITCH WATCHERS

WRITTEN BY
CHRISTOPHER BERRY

ILLUSTRATED BY EMILY HARPER

Visit www.christopherberryauthorvisits.com for information about Christopher's books, and how you can book a visit from Christopher in your school.

First published in Great Britain in 2014 by Christopher Berry and Emily Harper.

Printed in the UK by Lulu.com

ISBN 978-1-326-03267-8

For Katie
Because we've grown up loving Christmas together,
and it wouldn't be the same without you

THE EAST PUDDING CHRONICLES
Plight of the Witch Watchers

Chapter One
Granny Tells a Story

It was December 1st and in the village of Dandiest Pug, people were putting up their decorations and Christmas trees to mark the start of the festive season. At Number One, Cherry Street, George and Georgina were helping their Mum and Dad make the house sparkle and shimmer with lights and colour.

"Dipstick, stop eating the tinsel!" shouted Mum. The naughty pup reluctantly pulled his nose out of the tinsel box.

When Dipstick wasn't trying to eat it, Dad was adorning picture frames, mirrors and the rims of tables with thick, bushy, twinkling tinsel. He stuck George and Georgina's advent calendars on the kitchen door, ready for the first door to be opened that day. Then he stuck all the Christmas cards they had received along the banisters, going up the stairs. On the mantelpiece he placed a battery-operated Santa Claus, who would jiggle his arms and wiggle his bottom to the tune of *Jingle Bells*.

But Mum – with George and Georgina's help – was doing the most important job.

The Christmas tree.

George and Georgina didn't know why it was the most important decoration of all. They just knew that it was. Dad and Georgina went out earlier that day to Mrs Carnation's Christmas Tree Shop and bought a beautiful fir tree. This fir tree now stood, tall and majestic, in a big, red plant pot in the corner of George and Georgina's living room. It was by the living room window, so that people walking past could see it. Mum was very proud of her Christmas tree, so she was keen to show it off. She believed hers was the best in the village.

It was always Mum's job to put up the Christmas tree. The fact that George and Georgina were helping was new. Mum usually didn't let anyone touch her Christmas tree. She was very particular about it. It had to be just right, and only Mum knew how to get it just right. But George and Georgina had begged to help her, swaying her with sweet smiles, strawberry Quality Streets and cups of tea. So Mum gave in.

George had to sift through the tinsel box and pick out all the pink and blue tinsel. Mum chose different colours every year. Last year was red and gold. The year before that was blue and silver.

Georgina was tasked with untangling the fairy lights – white, twinkling, electric lights on long strands. This took nearly half an hour because clumsy Dipstick kept walking through them and getting stuck in them.

When the fairy lights were untangled, Georgina started draping them across the Christmas tree.

"No! Not yet!" cried Mum.

"Oh! Why? What are we missing?" asked Georgina.

"Oh, goodness me! Darling, how many times have you watched me put up the Christmas tree? The fairy always goes on first!"

"Oh, yes! The fairy needs to go on the top!" Georgina remembered. She darted over to the box that was labelled *The Christmas Fairy*. She lifted out a large, beautiful fairy with white, shining wings and a pink and blue, cone-shaped dress trimmed with silver. Georgina was quite a bit shorter than the Christmas tree, so she gave the fairy to Mum, and Mum perched her on top of the tree.

"That's better," said Mum. "First the fairy, then the fairy lights."

"Wait," said George, now sorting through all the baubles to find the pink and blue ones. "Don't some people put stars on their Christmas trees instead of fairies?"

"Yes, they do, George," explained Mum. "But that's a mistake people have been making for years. You see, fairies glow. They sparkle like bright lights. So from a distance, a Christmas tree with a fairy on top looked like a Christmas tree with a star on top."

"Oh, so people mistook the fairies for stars?"

"That's right."

After the fairy was on top, Georgina helped Mum drape the lights over the tree. Mum arranged them carefully so that every branch sparkled with a little light. Then both George and Georgina helped her decorate the tree with tinsel, baubles, chocolates and candy canes.

Mum had a habit of rearranging everything her children had just done. For example, when George placed a strand of tinsel, Mum took it off and moved it up a branch, always saying sweetly, "George, that looks lovely, but I tell you what. How about we try it here instead?" When Georgina hung a bauble, Mum would move it and hang it on a different branch, saying, "Sweety, that looks wonderful there, but do you think it might look more wonderful on this branch? I think so."

When the tree was done, Dad brought each of the three workers a nice cup of tea, and Dipstick a chew. (He was already getting curious about all the delightful smells of candy and chocolate now coming from the Christmas tree.)

But George and Georgina were curious about what they had just done.

12

"Why do we have Christmas trees?" asked George.

"Yes, and why do we put fairies and fairy lights on them and decorate them?" asked Georgina.

"And why do we put presents under them?" asked George.

"Oh dear!" cried Mum, smiling. "Where's your Granny when you need her?!"

"Don't you know?" said Georgina.

"I do, but I think I'll let your Granny tell you the story. She tells it better than me."

On Christmas Eve, Granny came to babysit the children while Mum and Dad were out for their Christmas Eve drinks. George, Georgina and Granny were all sat in the living room, eating cookies and watching *Home Alone II: Lost in New York*. They got to the bit at the end where Macaulay Culkin went to see the biggest Christmas tree in the whole of New York at the Rockefeller Centre, because of how much he loved Christmas trees. At that moment, Georgina glanced over at their Christmas tree, the fairy on top smiling, wings glinting, and remembered the questions they needed to ask Granny.

"Granny, why do we have Christmas trees?" she asked. "Why do we put fairies on top of them and decorate them with tinsel, baubles and fairy lights? And why do we put presents under them?"

"My loves," Granny whispered, "I've been waiting for

you to ask those questions. Shall I tell you how the Christmas tree began?"

"Yes, yes, yes!" George and Georgina peeped together.

"Well, it all started in East Pudding," Granny said. "It happened a number of years before what happened to the Twinkles, to Mrs Mistle and to Atnas. This is a story about the East Pudding Witch Watchers..."

Chapter 2
Mumble's Good Idea Day

Mumble did not trust Murmur. Mumble was the good wizard who ruled over East Pudding and Murmur was the evil witch who once ruled over West Pudding. Now her cold, stone castle was surrounded by the gnarled trees of Pudding Woods, and her cold, stone heart beat with nothing but hate. In her dungeons she plotted against Mumble and the residents of East Pudding, determined to bring an end to their Christmases.

Mumble could be a little dim-witted at times, forgetting where he put things, losing his train of thought and getting jams in his thinking cogs – as he put it. But one day, he came up with such a good idea that everyone in his castle threw a party to celebrate. They called it 'Mumble's Good Idea Day'. Chirrup the alarm clock made music with different alarm clock sounds, and the rabbits from Mumble's garden danced. Bumfy the comfy flying chair played musical chairs with Drop the

15

cookie jar, Bristler the broom and Mable the table. And the saucepan sisters, Alumi and Copps, prepared delicious chocolate custard with help from Birch the wooden spoon.

The good idea Mumble had had was that he was going to recruit a team of Witch Watchers to spy on Murmur. They would keep an eye on Murmur and feed back to Mumble whatever terrible deeds she might be planning, so that he and the rest of East Pudding could be ready.

"And where will you find these Witch Watchers, Mumble?" asked Alumi, sitting on Mumble's lap while he scooped chocolate custard out of her head.

"I need to find watchers I can trust, watchers I know can do the job, but they also need to be small – tiny – and unnoticeable," replied Mumble, with chocolate all around his mouth. "Murmur must never discover them. She must never know that they're there. I think I will have to sail across Yule Sea to the island of Dapple Crumples."

Copps, whose chocolate custard was being enjoyed by Dud, the fattest rabbit in Mumble's gardens, raised an eyebrow. "Do you mean Crumple Dimples?" she asked.

"That's what I said," replied Mumble. "Dipple Cramples."

"Whoopeee!" squealed Alumi. "Yaaay! Can we come?! Say we can come! I've always wanted to go to Crumple Dimples!"

"No, Alumi, you can't go," said Mumble sadly.

16

"I'm sorry. But Dample Crimples is a land of natural magic. You can't mix natural magic and wizard magic. You are alive because I brought you to life with my magic. But all the creatures on the island are born from magic. If I took you or

17

your sister there, you'd both turn back into regular saucepans."

"Well that's just a load of Bumfy fluff," Alumi huffed miserably.

"Sorry, girls!" Mumble chirruped. "Bumfy, you will be coming with me, of course. I need you to fly me to my boat on Yule Sea. But when we get to Crumple Dumples, you'll need to stay on the boat. Can't have you turning back into a regular chair."

"Mmmm ggggrr flllaaa aarr bbbbrrr," Bumfy gurgled.

"Oh, sorry, old friend." Mumble forgot that he was sitting on Bumfy. He leaned forwards.

"I said," Bumfy repeated, "you always seem to forget that when you sit on me and lean back, I cannot talk – or breathe!"

Mumble chuckled impishly. "Ooops! Sorry. I thought you were in a bit of sulk anyway after Mable beat you at musical chairs!"

"I was NOT sulking – because she did NOT beat me!" Bumfy protested. "I always win at musical chairs! I *am* a chair!"

"Not this time, Bumfy!" shouted Mable the table from the other side of the throne room. "It's time for you to take a back seat. Oh! See what I did there! Hahaha!"

"Mable..." said Mumble disapprovingly, wagging a

finger at the cheeky table. "Where are your table manners?"

"Yeah, Mable," shouted Bumfy. "Go break a leg!"

"Bumfy!" scolded Mumble.

After the festivities for Mumble's Good Idea Day drew to a close, Mumble packed some things for his trip to Crumple Dimples – a toothbrush, jelly babies and some cheese. Then Bumfy flew him across the kingdom to his boat on Yule Sea. Mumble had to leave his wand behind because it was powered by wizard magic. If he stepped onto Crumple Dimples with it, the natural magic on the island would turn it back into a stick.

Meanwhile, Murmur was in her castle, growing more and more suspicious. In the ripples of her cauldron, she had seen Mumble flying away on Bumfy. She had seen him celebrating with his castle friends, and the big banner hanging in his throne room proclaiming, 'Mumble's Good Idea Day'. Unfortunately for her, the mystical powers of the slurping red liquid in her cauldron only allowed her to *see* things that were happening, not *hear* them. All she knew was that something was afoot.

Now that Mumble and Bumfy had flown out of the cauldron's range, she couldn't see them either.

"What's this good idea of his, I wonder?" she snarled. "It's probably something ridiculous – just like he is. Bulbous!" She clicked her fingers and her chief vulture, Bulbous, flew across the dungeon towards her. "Follow that wizard. I want to know exactly what he's up to..."

Chapter Three
BooBoos and Flandingos

When Mumble arrived at Crumple
Dimples, he stepped out of his boat
onto purple sand. It was the only place
in the kingdom where you could find
purple sand, because it wasn't actually
sand. It was the Winnipeas – millions of tiny, purple insects
which were no bigger than grains of sand and liked to nibble
on people's feet. You wouldn't want to go paddling along the
shores of Crumple Dimples! Mumble made sure he kept his
shoes on.

Crumple Dimples was a truly magical
place, where flying pigs literally grew
on trees. Yes, literally! Magical
hollow trees
grew coconuts
that would,
once fully
grown, hatch
baby flying
pigs called
BooBoos. These pigs had the ability to
make wishes come true.

Mumble walked across
the 'sand', passing the magical
lighthouse that overlooked the
island from its southern edge. It
contained a set of doors and if
you passed through them, you

would travel inside the brains of the Brollies, a race of creatures that looked like miniature umbrellas.

The queen of Crumple Dimples was Troglup the Flandingo, an invisible dragon who lived in the castle at the centre of the island. Mumble journeyed there to speak with her.

"I request an audience with Troglup the Flandingo!" Mumble announced when he arrived at the gate of her castle, which was opened by a grumpy-looking, upside-down goblin. The goblin led Mumble through the  castle door into a grassy courtyard.

"Ah, there you are, Troglup," said Mumble quietly to himself, smirking.

Troglup was invisible, but Mumble could tell she was there. For one, he could hear her. She kept sneezing. For another, he could see the surging jets of fire blown from her nostrils each time she sneezed.

"Your Majesty, may I present... urm, what was your name again?" said the upside-down goblin.

"Mumble the wizard, ruler of East Pudding," Mumble whispered in reply.

"Mumble the wizard, ruler of East Pudding!" the goblin repeated for the queen. "And Mumble the wizard, ruler of East Pudding, may I present Her Majesty, Queen Troglup, Daughter of Mufflefluffbunch, Dragon Queen of Crumple Dimples and Thirteenth Heir of the House Flandingo."

"Do I need to remember all that?" Mumble asked with a pinch of worry.

"Mumble, my old friend!" boomed Troglup excitedly in her enormous voice, making the ground quake underfoot. "It's been a long – a-ah-ahh-AHCHOOO!"

Troglup sneezed all over her goblin, setting him on fire. As this had now happened a few times, several other goblins were on hand with buckets of water. They threw two buckets over him, putting out the fire, leaving him drenched, a little charred and even grumpier than he was before. A vast cloud of black smoke expanded around him.

"Ooops! That keeps happening today!" said Troglup, stepping through the huge cloud of smoke towards Mumble. As she did so, the grand, gigantic shape of a dragon was formed in the smoke.

Not wanting to be set on fire himself, Mumble took a few steps back.

"So my friend, what can I do for you?" Troglup roared.

"I'm looking to recruit some Witch Watchers, Troglup," said Mumble. "I want them to spy on Murmur, the witch who used to rule over West Pudding. I want to know what she's up to. So I need these Witch Watchers to be trustworthy, and I also need them to be small and unnoticeable. Murmur must never find out they are watching her."

"Mmmmm. Yes, I heard about that nasty business with West Pudding," said Troglup. "I agree she needs someone keeping an eye on her."

"Any suggestions?" Mumble asked.

"Well, let me see. I don't think the BooBoos would be much use to you. They're too big and well, they're pigs. They fart a lot and they smell. They do grant wishes, but only three. So, you see, you could wish them to be silent, invisible and not smelly – but that would take all your wishes. You couldn't then wish them to be spies."

"Ah, I see," said Mumble.

Troglup had another thought. "There's the Winnipeas. They're the tiniest living things on the island. Oh, but wait. I don't know how much you could trust them. They're just hungry insects, after all. The Brollies wouldn't be any good to you, either. They're small and unnoticeable in dry weather, but as soon as it rains, they open up."

Mumble nodded. "Yes, I don't think the Brollies and the Winnipeas would make ideal Witch Watchers..."

"Ah! I know!" cried Troglup suddenly. "My fleas!"

"Your fleas?"

"Yes! Well, they're invisible – like me! And they're very intelligent and loyal. They'd make great spies. Oh no, wait. That won't work either. As soon as they smell oranges, they start losing their memories. If I remember correctly, lots of juicy orange smells waft across East Pudding from the Orange Grove."

Mumble shook his head. "Oh. Yes, they do. That won't work, then."

"That leaves one option, my friend," said Troglup

hopefully. "Fairies. They're loyal, intelligent, small and unnoticeable – as long as they turn off their glow. No one would see or hear them."

"Sounds like they'd make perfect spies," Mumble agreed.

"Fandabbydozy. I will speak to some of the fairy families. Wait here."

Apart from the sound of giant wings flapping, Mumble would not have been able to tell that Troglup had just flown away from the castle. That is – until she soared straight through a white, puffy cloud hanging over the castle, leaving a dragon-shaped hole in the centre of it.

Chapter Four
The Fairy Celeste

A short while later, Troglup returned. Following her in flight was a cluster of tiny stars, one brighter than the rest.

The little stars landed on the grass at Mumble's feet, at which point he saw that they weren't stars at all. They were glowing fairies with pointy noses and ears, beautiful white wings and shining skin, hair and eyes. The one who shone brighter than the rest was older and much larger, though she still didn't reach Mumble's knee.

"Good day to you, Mumble," said the larger fairy. "My name is Celeste. These are my children. We will be your Witch Watchers."

Behind Celeste, her tiny, glowing children – each of them no bigger than a thumb – smiled at Mumble. There must have been nearly fifty of them!

"These are *all* your children?" Mumble gasped.

Celeste laughed. "Fairies have lots of children, Mumble. My sister has two hundred!"

"Jolly waffles!" cried Mumble. "Two hundred?!"

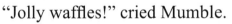

Suddenly, Celeste's expression changed. Her warm smile twisted into a frown. "Oh dear," she whispered dreadfully. "I've spotted a flaw in our plan to spy on this wicked witch of yours."

"What flaw?" asked Mumble.

Celeste pointed. "It appears she's already spying on us."

Mumble turned around, following the direction of her tiny, glowing finger. She was pointing towards the sky, where a sinister black vulture was hovering, watching and listening intently. It was Bulbous. When Bulbous realized he had been spotted, he turned in the air quickly and started flying away.

"Oh no!" shrieked Mumble. "I don't have my wand! We have to stop it!"

"Don't panic," said Celeste calmly. "I have mine."

Celeste unveiled her wand and pointed it at Bulbous. A sharp pink light shot out of the tip and streaked across the sky, electrocuting the fleeing vulture. Dead, he plummeted into the coconut trees. He knocked several coconuts off their branches as he fell, causing a number of BooBoos to hatch a little earlier than they had planned.

"Well, that was easy," muttered Celeste.

"Go, Mummy!" squeaked a number of her children, squeaky as baby mice.

"Very well done, Celeste," said Mumble, smiling. "I can see we're going to make a good team."

"I think so too," Celeste agreed. "Shall we be on our way to East Pudding?"

"Yes, let's," said Mumble. "Then the witch watching can begin."

"Good luck!" rumbled Troglup, as Mumble, Celeste and her children started out of the castle. "Good luck to ya-ah-ahh-AHCHOOO!"

Troglup sneezed again – and set another goblin on fire.

Chapter Five
Watch of the Witch Watchers

So began the watch of the Witch Watchers. Celeste and her children went to live in Pudding Woods near Murmur's castle. They turned off their glow so that nobody would notice them, any more than someone might notice a fly or bee. In fact, they were even less noticeable than that. Bees and flies have wings that make buzzing sounds. Fairies' wings were silent.

Their efforts as spies worked rather well. Celeste got her children to fly around the castle and listen by windows to the things going on inside. She got them to hide inside the castle, to linger in the cracks in the walls, the shadows in the corners of rooms, and hide beneath the feathers of Murmur's vultures. The fairies listened to the details of Murmur's dark plots and reported back to their mother. Celeste would then fly to Mumble's castle to inform him.

Murmur plotted the kidnap of joke-telling sweet-maker, Timothy Twinkle, and his toymaker husband, Tiberius Twinkle. But Celeste informed Mumble in time. Mumble was able to hide the Twinkles – temporarily shrinking them to the size of pennies and hiding them in jars – until Murmur gave up looking for them.

Then Murmur plotted to kill expert pie maker and flower lady, Mrs Mistle. But again, Celeste informed Mumble in time. The wizard temporarily turned the already half-plant Mrs Mistle into a fully-fledged flower.

One day, shortly after both her plans had failed, Murmur was pacing up and down her throne room in a rage. She was flicking lightning bolts from her fingertips, accidentally zapping a couple of her vultures and making them POOF! into a scattering of feathers.

"I will have that wizard strangled by a hundred snakes when I get my hands on him!" she roared.

One of Celeste's children, a little boy fairy called Warren, was hiding in the shadow of Murmur's throne, listening.

"It is true, Your Majesty," said Mr Weenie, a tall, thin man and Murmur's most loyal servant. "It is true that Mumble seems to know what we are going to do before we do it. He appears to be ahead of us at every turn."

"There's something going on here," Murmur realized. "That wizard isn't clever enough to just guess my plans, nor does he have the ability to see into the future. So how can he know?"

"There is mystery all around us, I fear, Your Majesty," said Mr Weenie, with gloom and dread in his voice. "Mystery and deception. There are things we cannot see that are right in front of our noses."

Warren swallowed hard. No one in the room could see him, because he was tiny and completely hidden by shadow. But now he felt like *everyone* could see him.

"And what of Bulbous?" Murmur remembered. "We still do not know what happened to him. I sent him away to find out what Mumble was up to – and he disappeared."

"Like I say, Your Majesty. Mystery and deception all around."

"Well I've had enough." Murmur stood up. Her vultures cowered – in fear that her fiery temper might ignite again. "Mr Weenie, I want you to find out what is going on. NOW."

"Yes, Your Majesty."

As soon as Mr Weenie left the throne room, when Murmur's back was turned, Warren flew silently out of the shadows and through the nearest open window.

He flew as fast as he could through the trees, panicked.

I must get home to Mother, the little fairy thought desperately. Murmur's onto us!

He flew so fast – his head in such a tiz-woz – that he wasn't looking where he was going and flew straight into a tree.

32

He didn't knock himself out, but he accidentally turned on his glow. Not realizing it was on, Warren took off again and resumed his speedy flight through the woods.

What he didn't know was that Mr Weenie was only a few metres behind him. Straight away, Mr Weenie noticed what looked like a bright, tiny star winding its way through the trees at high speeds.

Mr Weenie smirked evilly. Murmur will be so pleased with me! he thought proudly.

He hurried back to the castle and darted up the cockroach-covered staircase to Murmur's throne room.

"Mr Weenie!" said Murmur, her dark eyes wide with surprise. "Back already? What have you found?"

"I've found the truth, Your Majesty," said Mr Weenie, breathless after his run up the stairs. "We are being watched. We're being watched.... by fairies."

Chapter Six
Warren's Mistake

"Mother! Mother!" Warren bawled as he flew towards his family's home inside a huge, hollow log called the Great Tunnel Tree.

"Sssshhh!" scolded Celeste, flying out of the Great Tunnel Tree to greet him. "Seventeen of your sisters are asleep!"

"But Mother, I have news!" Warren gasped.

"Warren – why are you glowing?" Celeste asked.

"What? I'm not!"

"Yes, you are! Look!" Celeste grabbed Warren's arm and flew him to a small puddle by the Great Tunnel Tree.

Warren threw his hand over his mouth in shock when he saw his glowing reflection in the puddle. "Oh no!!"

"Oh, Warren... what have you done?"

Suddenly, a great wind whipped through the trees with the force of a Giant's sneeze. Hissing bolts of lightning ripped

past branches and bushes, frying and scattering leaves and
bits of wood. Flying
towards Celeste and
Warren on the back
of one of her vultures
was Murmur,
surrounded by sparks
and flashes of
crackling lightning.

The vulture
landed just before the
Great Tunnel Tree,
where Celeste and
Warren looked on in horror. Murmur climbed off the vulture's
back, wielding her magic wand, which looked like a crooked
tree root. Her face was warped with rage.

"So... I have you to thank for the recent failure of all my
great plans," Murmur hissed. "Well, your little surveillance
operation is at an end."

"Careful, Murmur," Celeste said boldly, trying to hide her terror. "We have magic, too."

"Hahaha!" Murmur cackled. "I am a witch! Do you seriously think I fear the magic of... a fairy?"

"We are from Crumple Dimples, the land of natural magic, ruled over by the most powerful dragon who's ever lived – Queen Troglup the Flandingo. You would be wise to leave us alone."

"Ooooo!" Murmur cried in mock fear, pretending to shake. "I quiver at the thought of Queen Troglup. If Queen Troglup was here, I'd be eating dragon pie by now."

"Trust me. You don't want to do this."

"Don't I? Draw your wand, fairy. We'll see if natural magic is a match for witch magic."

"Mother, don't..." Warren whispered.

"It's all right, Warren. Go inside. Be with your brothers and sisters," replied Celeste.

Warren flew inside the Great Tunnel Tree. "What's happening?" asked Weep, one of his sisters.

"We've been discovered," Warren replied dreadfully, shaking his head. "Murmur's found us – and it's my fault."

Celeste brandished her wand, pointing it at Murmur, her tiny wrist trembling. She fired a streak of pink lightning at the witch, but Murmur deflected it with her own wand, returning fire with a sharp surge of black lightning.

The pink and black lightning bolts clawed at one another in mid-air like hands. But the black lightning was stronger. The pink lightning was shrinking, arching towards Celeste as it buckled under the weight of Murmur's powers.

SNAP!

The black lightning defeated the pink, pushed Celeste backwards, and tossed her magic wand out of her hand.

Regaining her strength, Celeste started to fly over to where the wand had fallen to retrieve it. But Murmur charged at Celeste and grabbed her, clasping her hand tightly around the fairy's waist.

"I told you you were no match for me," Murmur hissed.

Still holding Celeste, she pinched the little fairy's wings in her fingers and viciously ripped them off.

Celeste screamed. At that moment, her children flew out of the Great Tunnel Tree to find out what was happening to their mother.

Murmur threw Celeste – now wingless – to the ground. Murmur let go of her wings and watched them flutter by themselves in the air, directionless without Celeste to guide them. Murmur used her wand to steer the wings' flight path. She steered them towards a nearby fir tree.

Injured and weak, Celeste struggled to her feet. She watched as her own wings flew up the fir tree and landed on the pointy branch at the top, as far from her reach as they could be.

"Mother! Your wings!" squeaked Peep, another one of Celeste's daughters.

"I'll get them for you, Mother!" shouted Warren, heroically flying towards the fir tree.

"No, you won't!" Murmur snarled. A spark of lightning surged from the tip of her wand and seared into Warren, burning his wings off his back. With a tiny splash, one that barely produced a ripple, he dropped into a puddle on the forest floor.

Murmur did the same with all the other fairy children. She rained down sparks of lightning from her wand on all of them, burning away their wings.

Now none of the fairies were able to fly. And being so small, it was going to take days for them to walk back to East Pudding.

Murmur grinned wickedly. "I shall leave you to think about what you've done. And I trust you never to cross me again."

She turned and her vast, black cape waved and swirled like the eye of a storm. She climbed onto the back of her vulture and flew first to where Celeste's wand had fallen. She picked it up and tucked it inside her cloak. Then she flew back through the trees to her castle, leaving the fairies wingless, helpless and magic-less.

Chapter Seven
Wings

"Mother, what are we going to do?" squealed Weep. "We have no magic! And no wings!"

"Don't panic, children," said Celeste comfortingly, but secretly unsure herself. "Here's what we're going to do. I'm going to climb to the top of that fir tree and get my wings back. Then I'll fly back to East Pudding and get help. And you'll wait here."

"No, Mother!" cried Warren, his little voice edged with worry. "You can't climb that fir tree by yourself! It's too tall! You'll never make it!"

"Shut up, you!" snapped Weep. "You started this! Why didn't you realize your glow was on?!"

"Weep, stop it," Celeste commanded in a deep voice. "He panicked. It was a mistake. We all make mistakes."

"Not ones that get our wings burned off!" Weep continued to argue.

"I'm sorry," Warren whispered, starting to cry. "I said I was sorry. I don't know what else to say."

"All right, everyone calm down," said Celeste. "Warren has said he's sorry. And you're all going to forgive him. Because any of you might have done the same thing. And that'll be the end of it. Okay?"

"Yes, Mother," said all of her children together. Weep still looked angry – probably more upset – but she said it too.

"Right, I'm going to climb that fir tree," said Celeste, bravely taking the deepest breath she had ever taken.

She approached the fir tree. She could see her wings stuck at the top, fluttering gently in the breeze that wisped through the woods. They looked so far away.

If only I was a bit bigger! she thought.

She climbed onto the first branch. The tree's needle-like leaves prickled her legs and made them itch. She carried on up.

When she got a quarter of the way up, she stopped and took some deep breaths. She was exhausted. You see, fairies never climbed. They never needed to. They could fly. But worse than that, a lot of fairies' strength was in their wings. They were weaker without them – another reason why Celeste was so exhausted.

But if Celeste ever hoped to fly again, she had to climb. She had no choice.

She reached up and grabbed the next prickly branch, pulling herself up.

Celeste climbed and climbed, while her children watched at the bottom, all with anxious looks on their faces.

When Celeste was halfway up, she stopped again for a rest. She looked down below. Her children looked blurry to her now. Her eyes were getting heavy. She was getting more and more worn-out.

She looked up. Her wings were still there at the top, fluttering in the breeze.

"Oooh, why must you still be so far away..." Celeste whispered sadly to herself.

Even though her whole body ached, she continued to climb.

"Mother, are you okay?" Warren called to her.

Celeste stopped. "Y-yes! I – I'm fine, Warren!" she cried breathlessly, lying. She didn't turn round. She just kept climbing.

"I don't know if I believe her," whispered Warren to his brothers and sisters. "She's worn-out. She's getting slower and slower."

"She'll make it," said Pickle hopefully, one of Warren's brothers.

Celeste stopped again. She could barely breathe. Her tiny heart pounded. Every tiny muscle in her body throbbed.

She looked up. She was so near the top now.

But her eyes were getting heavier and heavier.

She carried on, reaching for the next branch, and lifting

herself onto it. She could hardly feel the prickles of the bristly leaves anymore. Her legs were almost numb.

Finally! she thought, as she climbed onto the final branch at the top, just next to the pointy branch her wings were attached to.

She reached out to grab her wings and detach them from the branch.

But just then, a much larger wind gusted through the woods. In a cruel twist of fate, the wind caught Celeste's wings and blew them off the pointy branch.

Celeste jumped, leaping towards the wings, stretching to grab them.

She missed.

As her children watched in horror from below, the fierce wind carried her wings into the sky, until they were completely out of sight.

Gone.

Celeste, weak and weary, slumped miserably against the pointy branch.

"Mother!" cried Weep. "What are you going to do now?"

"I – I don't know, my – my darling," Celeste called down to her, between breaths. "But I – I don't think I've – I've got the energy to get back down this – this tree."

"We have to go up there for her," said Warren to his brothers and sisters. "All of us. We have to go up there and help her down. She needs us."

"Agreed," said Peep and Weep together. "All of us. Let's go."

"W-what – are you all whispering about down – down there?" shouted Celeste.

"We're coming to help you down, Mother!" said Warren.

"No, son! D-d-don't! I – I –!" Celeste's eyes now felt so heavy that it was as though her eyelids were made of fairinium, even pixinium. (These were types of metal that fairies produced on Crumple Dimples. Fairinium was heavy. Pixinium was even heavier.)

Celeste's children ignored their mother's warning and started climbing the fir tree. Some of the fairy children were faster than others, but it wasn't long before all of them started feeling the effects of the climb – complete and utter exhaustion.

"I – I don't know how much longer I can – can do this!" shouted Pickle, gasping for air.

"Everything hurts!"

"I – I know!" squealed Weep. "I can barely breathe!"

"Children, please!" shouted Celeste from the top. "Pl-please – go back down!"

"We can't! You need us!" Warren shouted back. He was halfway up the tree with three of his brothers and seven of his sisters, but he was quickly getting worn-out. Six of his sisters and five of his brothers were ahead of him, but they were getting slower and slower.

The children, being so tiny, had even less energy than their mother. But they were so determined to help her that they wouldn't stop climbing. Even though their little bodies were wearing out fast, they refused to stop.

Three of Celeste's children were able to climb onto the cluster of branches just below her. Pickle, Bubble and Raindrop.

"My darlings...." Celeste whispered to them.

But Pickle, Bubble and Raindrop had stopped. They just couldn't climb anymore. Their bodies had given up. They looked up at their mother.

"We can't, Mother," they whispered, their faces sad and tired. "We can't go on."

Celeste knew that her children were dying. She knew that she was dying, too.

At that moment, she had an idea. Something they could all do. Something that might save them, or it might not. Nothing was certain, and it was something no fairy had done for centuries.

Hibernate. Hibernate and recharge.

"My darling boys and girls..." she called to her children.

They were spread out across the tree, but now all of them had stopped climbing. Some were near the top, some were only halfway, and some were still near the bottom.

"My darlings, listen to me," Celeste continued. "We're going to hibernate. We're going to fall into the deepest sleep and recharge our energy. It's the only way."

"But M-Mother," murmured Pickle breathlessly. "Hibernation is – is dangerous. I read that many fairies never wake up again..."

"It's true," Celeste confirmed. "We may never wake up. But it's the only chance we've got."

"We love you, Mother," whispered Warren, who had managed to climb until he was three quarters of the way up. But he had stopped too, unable to go on.

As his whisper carried on the wind, brushing gently past him at that moment, Warren closed his eyes. Following his mother's command, he fell into a deep, deep sleep.

Pickle, Bubble and Raindrop closed their eyes and did the same. So, too, did Weep and Peep, and all the rest of their brothers and sisters.

Once she saw that her children had closed their eyes and slipped into a deep, peaceful, dreamless sleep, Celeste closed hers and joined them, with a smile on her lips.

As they went into hibernation, each fairy started to glow. But it wasn't their full glow. It wasn't bright and constant. It was more of a gentle, blinking glow. A twinkle. It showed that they were recharging.

As the darkest night of all time fell over Pudding Woods, the fairies twinkled like tiny, flickering lights all across the fir tree, with Celeste at the top glimmering like a star.

Chapter Eight
Which Witch Watchers?

Dud, the fattest rabbit in Mumble's gardens, had been appointed by Mumble to pay occasional visits to the fairies. His job was to see if they were all right, and to see if they needed anything.

But this time, when he visited Celeste and her children at the Great Tunnel Tree, he wasn't expecting to find the huge fallen log empty – with no trace of the fairies.

Dud looked around. He called out to them, but there was no answer. He checked beneath the Great Tunnel Tree, looked for burrows in the ground and checked underneath a few nearby bushes. But when he found nothing, he started back to East Pudding, sad and confused.

He didn't look hard enough. Because he didn't notice the huge fir tree glowing with lights a short distance away.

Dud hopped back to Mumble's castle and bounced up the steps to his throne room.

"Mumble, they're gone!" he squeaked. "The Witch Watchers are gone!"

"Which Witch Watchers?" asked Mumble, one eyebrow raised in befuddlement.

"No, the Witch Watchers," said Dud.

"Yes, but which Witch Watchers?"

"No, no. Not Witch Witch Watchers," explained Dud. "Just Witch Watchers."

"Huh?" cried Mumble, scratching his head. "What on earth are you talking about, you big buffoon?!"

"Oh! You mean *which* Witch Watchers?" wondered Dud.

"No," said Mumble. "I mean Witch Watchers, not Witch Witch Watchers."

At last, Bristler the broom whacked Mumble across the head with a loud DONK. "For the love of custard tarts, Mumble! The fairies! Dud means the fairies!"

"What? The fairies are gone, Dud?" gasped Mumble.

"I'm afraid so, Mumble," said Dud sadly. "I called to them. Nothing. I looked around for them. Nothing...."

"Mumble! Mumble!" cried Ernie the pigeon as he flew into the throne room through the window. It was Tuesday, and Ernie would come to sing to Mumble on Tuesdays.

Except that this time he brought news instead. Sad news.

"What is it, Ernie?" Mumble asked.

"I'm sorry, Mumble," said Ernie glumly. "But when I flew to the Orange Grove this morning, I found these. They'd landed in the grass, in a clearing near the edge of Pudding Woods. I spotted them twinkling from the sky."

Ernie opened out his grey, feathered wings, revealing a pair of very different sorts of wings. Delicate, thin and see-though, like fine pieces of lace, and glinting with fairy dust. They were fairy wings. But with no fairy attached.

"Oh my! Are those the wings of the fairy Celeste?" cried Mumble.

"It looks that way," said Ernie.

Mumble put his head in his hands. "Murmur. Murmur must've got to them. Oh, the poor fairies. I should never have asked them to be Witch Watchers."

"We can hope that Murmur gave them quick deaths," said Bristler.

"Yes," said Mumble. "We can hope."

Chapter Nine
Podney Tiptoe

A few years later, on the night before Christmas Eve, a little boy called Podney Tiptoe was dashing through Pudding Woods, as fast as his little legs could carry him.

Chasing after him was Murmur's chief vulture, Venom, who had replaced Bulbous after his disappearance. Venom had a long history of serving witches.

Years ago, he used to serve a witch called Xenia in a faraway land called Jemwar. But then something happened. During a clifftop battle between Xenia and her enemies, Venom was pulled inside a strange tunnel in the sky and dragged into another world altogether. He ended up in West Pudding, where he was taken in by Murmur.

The journey through the tunnel left half of his body covered in scales instead of feathers – like a snake. He was so frightening to look at, that if ever Murmur needed someone to chase after a little boy or girl, Venom was her first choice.

This particular little boy – Podney – had not done anything wrong, but he had gotten too close to Murmur's castle. His Mum and Dad had told him stories about the Witch Watchers and their disappearance, and he was curious. He wanted to see if he could find the lost fairies and bring them home in time for Christmas.

When Murmur saw Podney traipsing through Pudding Woods that evening, she sent Venom to capture him. Christmas was when she was at her most miserable – and least merciful.

She fancied a spot of Little Boy Pie.

Podney charged through the woods, his feet beginning to ache. He hoped that he was heading towards East Pudding. But it was getting dark and cold and he was struggling to see where he was going.

He came across the Great Tunnel Tree, which his parents had told him used to be the home of the fairies. But it wasn't time to start hunting for clues. He needed to hide from Venom.

He wondered if he could fit inside the Great Tunnel Tree, which was a hollow log. But he quickly realized he was too big. He looked around for something else to hide in or under.

Then he saw something. Lights.

Sparkling lights shining through the trees. In the last few years, everything around the Great Tunnel Tree had become really overgrown. Big bushes and tall weeds had grown up everywhere. The trees had bent inwards, becoming twisted and tangled together, looking like a giant, crooked cobweb. Probably Murmur's evil infecting the woods. That was why Podney didn't notice the lights at first.

When he heard the flap of vulture wings a short distance away, he veered towards the lights, carving through the bushes and brambles.

WOW, he thought when he saw it.

A tall fir tree was adorned with lots of tiny white lights. A silvery light – the biggest of them all – shimmered at the very top.

It's a magical tree! he decided.

The flap of wings got closer. Podney went up to the tree. He looked and realized there was space to crawl beneath it. So he got down on his knees and crept underneath, tucking himself behind the lowest branches and hugging the trunk. He waited for Venom to appear.

Finally, the hideous half-snake vulture emerged from between the trees. He immediately noticed the huge fir tree, all lit up and glowing. But underneath the tree, Podney was wrapped in shadow. Venom didn't see him.

"Come out, little boy..." Venom hissed evilly. "Murmur only wants to eat you. I've known her to do worse things than that..."

Venom flew closer to the fir tree, curious about the lights. Suddenly, a rustling noise a few metres away made him spin fast in the air, thinking it was Podney.

But it was only a toad, who had jumped through some bushes and onto a lily pad in a puddle.

Venom was about to fly away and continue searching for Murmur's tasty dessert, when possibly the unluckiest thing to ever happen to Podney happened. And it happened at the worst possible moment.

He sneezed.

Venom turned his horrible furless head, twitched his orange beak and glared at the fir tree. He flew close to the ground and peered hard into the darkness beneath the tree. There in the shadows, he was just about able to make out Podney's frightened face.

"Ah ha!" cried Venom triumphantly. "Well played, you little urchin. Hiding right under my beak. Well, now the game's over."

Venom approached the tree. Podney tried not to move, but he was trembling, breathing fast and his heart was pounding hard.

This is it, thought Podney. He's got me.

Venom flew close to the tree. He was about to stretch his neck beneath it and grab Podney in his beak, when one of the tiny lights on the lower branches started glowing brighter. It distracted Venom for a second, making him squint, but he ignored it and tried to reach Podney again.

Podney didn't move. There was nowhere to left to run.

"Come here, you little rat!" snarled Venom.

The vulture was just about to snap his beak around Podney's wrist, when a few more of the lights on the tree got brighter. Venom felt a wave of heat from the lights against his half-feathered, half-scaled back.

Venom moved away and looked up. Now every light – including the big light at the top – was shimmering and shining brighter than the sun. In mere moments, they had caused Venom to go blind.

And it was because Venom was now blind that he didn't see the powerful heat from the lights set fire to one of his wings. Well, not until he could smell singed feathers and feel the pain of the fire burning through to his skin.

"Aaarrrgggh!!" Venom shrieked, as the flames flared across his back. He flew away, searching desperately for water to put out the fire. Being blind made that a lot more difficult.

But luckily for Venom, being blind also caused him to fly straight into a tree and fall into a stream below. He rolled in the water quickly, drenching himself. The water strangled the flames and they fizzled away, leaving Venom with no feathers or fur, just scales and skin. Now he was both blind and even more hideous than he was before.

But at least he never had to look at his reflection again.

Chapter Ten
The First Christmas Tree

After Venom had flown away, the lights on the fir tree dimmed again, twinkling as they did before. The coast was clear, so Podney crawled out from beneath the tree, climbed to his feet and looked up.

It protected me, he thought, looking at the fir tree and smiling. The magical tree saved me.

He ran back to East Pudding to tell his parents about it.

Arriving home, Podney walked through his front door and into the hallway. He could hear his parents talking in the living room. Podney walked down the hall. He saw his parents

sat on the floor next to a big heap of wrapped Christmas presents, with rolls of wrapping paper, sticky tape and scissors in front of them.

"That's the last one," said Mrs Tiptoe, adding a package wrapped in gold paper to the heap of presents. "Everything's wrapped."

"Now what?" said Mr Tiptoe. "We've been invited to Mrs Carter's for Christmas Eve supper tomorrow. Where shall we put all these presents? There's a lot more here than last year."

"Mmmm," wondered Mrs Tiptoe. "We need to put them somewhere they'll be safe. Somewhere they'll be protected."

"I've got an idea," announced Podney from the living room doorway.

"Podney!" cried his mother. "I didn't see you there! Where have you been? And why are your cheeks so red?"

"I've been in Pudding Woods," he admitted. "Got chased by a vulture."

"Podney!!" snapped Mr Tiptoe. "We told you not to go looking for the Witch Watchers!"

"I know, but I had to. It's Christmas time. Ever since you told me about them, I've been thinking of them out there. Alone. Alone at Christmas."

"And did you find them?" asked Mrs Tiptoe.

Podney's head drooped. "No," he said gloomily. "I didn't. But I found something else."

"Oh?"

"Father, come with me. I've found something that'll protect our Christmas presents – just like it protected me. We'll need the largest wheelbarrow you've got. And an axe."

Intrigued, Mr Tiptoe followed his son to Pudding Woods, pushing the largest wheelbarrow he could find in his shed. Podney guided him through the trees, following the faint stream of light given off by the fir tree.

When they arrived at the tree, Mr Tiptoe's eyes widened and his mouth fell open in awe.

"Oh my days..." he whispered, enchanted by all the twinkling lights.

"It's a magical tree," said Podney. "I snuck underneath it, hiding from the vulture who was

trying to kidnap me and take me to Murmur. When the vulture found me, all the lights got brighter and hotter and set the vulture on fire."

Mr Tiptoe walked up to the tree for a closer look. Studying the lights up close, he realized something his son hadn't.

The lights were not actually lights. They were tiny fairies. Initially, because of their gentle twinkle, he couldn't tell they were fairies. They all looked like they were fast asleep.

Mr Tiptoe looked up. The biggest light at the top was also a sleeping fairy.

This isn't a magical tree, Mr Tiptoe thought to himself. Podney has found the lost fairies. He's found the Witch Watchers. He just hasn't realized it.

Mr Tiptoe presumed the fairies were dead. After all, they weren't moving. They weren't breathing. They went missing a few years ago, so they had probably been like this a while.

But then, what about Podney's story about the lights getting brighter and hotter and setting the vulture on fire?

In any case, he chose not to tell Podney that the lights were the lost fairies. He didn't want to upset him. He chose to let his son continue thinking that it was a magical tree.

"Let's take it home with us, Father," said Podney. "The tree isn't safe out here. Not in Pudding Woods. Not this close to Murmur's castle. The moment she realizes it's here, she'll destroy it."

"All right, son," said Mr Tiptoe. "We'll take it home."

Podney smiled as his father cut down the magical tree with his axe and lifted it into the wheelbarrow.

As they took the tree back through the woods, at one point, the wheelbarrow hit a small rock in the ground and jerked. One of the fairy children fell off the branches. Podney was about to go and pick it up when his father noticed. He stopped and dashed over to where the fairy had fallen, picking it up himself.

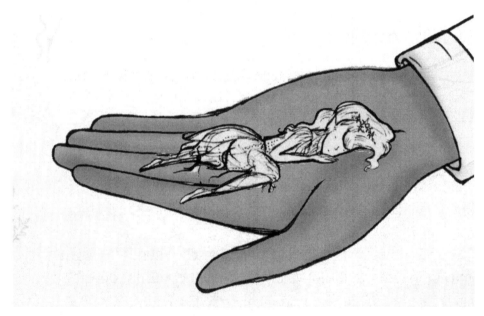

He placed the little fairy back onto its branch and they carried on back to the village.

When they got home, Mr Tiptoe took the fir tree into the living room and stood it in a plant pot in the corner of the room.

"There you are, Mother," said Podney, proudly looking

up at the tree. "Put all the presents under the tree. They'll be safe there. I promise."

"Wait? Are those...?" said Mrs Tiptoe to her husband, noticing that the lights were in fact not lights at all.

"Yes, sadly there are," whispered Mr Tiptoe. "But ssshhh... I didn't want to tell Podney the truth. It'll just upset him."

So Podney stayed blissfully unaware.

But Mr Tiptoe did go and tell Mumble that they had found his Witch Watchers, and he told him the story of how – even in death – they had saved his son from Murmur. He also told his neighbours in East Pudding.

The next day was Christmas Eve and Mumble and a number of residents in East Pudding came to visit the Tiptoes. Those residents included Mrs Carter, the Dumples, the Twinkles, Mr Jellylegs and Mr Jellyfingers, Mrs Bollybongo, Miss Bella-Swiss, Mr Ribbet and Mrs Mistle. They had come to see the Tiptoes' tree and pay their respects to the lost fairies.

From that moment on, every family in East Pudding started bringing fir trees into their living rooms at Christmas time. It was a way of remembering the lost fairies and how they gave their lives to protect East Pudding, and saved Podney from Murmur. They covered their trees in tiny, twinkling lights, which they called fairy lights. They put fairy dolls on top to represent Celeste. Just like the Tiptoes had, they placed their Christmas presents under their trees to protect them, reminding them of how the fairies had protected Podney.

Over time, other decorations came to join the fairy lights. Baubles. Beads. Tinsel. Ribbons. It was Timothy Twinkle's idea to hang chocolates from the branches, too.

The people of East Pudding celebrated their trees, made them beautiful, and turned them into the centrepiece of their living rooms at Christmas time.

And thereafter they became known as Christmas trees.

Chapter Eleven
Time for Bed

As Granny finished her story, George stared at her, eyes wide, mouth partly open, waiting for her to continue. When Granny said nothing, he screwed up his face into a frown. "Granny, wait a minute," he said. "Is that the end of the story?"

Granny looked at George blankly. "Yes, George. That's the end."

"No, Granny, it can't be the end," insisted George. "You haven't even told us what happened to the fairies!"

"Yeah, Granny!" Georgina chimed in. "Were they dead? Or were they still in hibernation?"

"Oh, I see," said Granny. "Well, that's something we'll never know..."

"WHAT?!" the children shouted in horror together.

"... For certain, anyway," Granny added.

"What do you mean, *for certain*?" asked Georgina.

Granny explained, "Well, the story of what happened to the very first Christmas tree is a bit hazy..."

"I don't care about haze!" cried George. "Give us haze!"

Granny laughed. "What I've heard is that after having the first Christmas tree in their house that Christmas, the Tiptoes donated it to Mumble. As to what happened next, well, there are two stories. Would you like both of them?"

"YES!" the children yelled together.

Granny grinned. "One says that each Christmas, Mumble put up the Christmas tree, and each year, one of the fairies would no longer twinkle, like the hibernation hadn't worked and the fairy had died. They say – strange as it sounds – that's why with the electric fairy lights we have on our trees today, there's always one bulb each year that stops working..."

"And the other story?" asked Georgina.

"The other story says that one Christmas, Mumble awoke to find the tree bare. The fairies had gone, and Mumble never saw them again."

"Gone? Gone where?"

"People say the hibernation worked and, though it took several years, the fairies had successfully managed to recharge themselves. Some say that in the time they took to hibernate, their wings regrew and they were able to fly back to Crumple Dimples. Others say they flew around the world. That the fairy children grew up and now they stand on the tops of Christmas trees all over the world. So next time you see a Christmas tree, take a close look at the fairy on the top, because it could be the real thing..."

George looked up at the fairy on top of their Christmas tree. Its smiling face, arms, legs and wings were as still as the night sky – frozen. "Oh, Granny, don't be silly!" laughed George. "All Christmas fairies are dolls! They're not real!"

"I'm sure you're right, George," Granny said.

"Well, which story is true?" Georgina asked.

"Which story would you like to be true, my love?"

George and Georgina looked at each other. Then they looked back at Granny, yelling together, "The second one, of course!!"

Granny smiled. "Then that is the story which is true."

"But Granny – you don't *know* what happened to the lost fairies?" George said with a worried look on his face.

"I'm afraid, my darling, your Granny doesn't know everything!" Granny chuckled.

"Could've fooled me!" cried George.

Granny leaned forwards in her armchair. "I do know one thing...." she whispered, as if she was about to tell a big secret, and she was afraid the walls might hear.

George and Georgina leaned in towards Granny. "What?" they asked together.

"I know it's time for bed!"

"Oh, Granny!" the children cried, disappointed.

"Come on now, children. Santa will be here soon."

With a sigh, George picked up Mrs Snuggles. Georgina wrapped her arms around Mr Snuggles. Dragging their feet, they clumped upstairs with their teddies and climbed into bed.

When the two children had left the living room, Granny glanced over at the Christmas tree. The fairy lights twinkled. The tinsel fluttered. The baubles glimmered. The fairy on top stared.

Granny wasn't surprised when the fairy winked at her.

She simply smiled and winked back.

OTHER BOOKS IN
THE EAST PUDDING CHRONICLES

The Christmas Monster

The Merry Mrs Mistle

Tale of the Twinkles

ABOUT THE AUTHOR

This latest book in *The East Pudding Chronicles* is the one that Christopher Berry was most excited to write. It's also the one he struggled with the most. The Christmas tree is probably the season's greatest tradition. How do you write an origin story that lives up to it? The real origins of the Christmas tree aren't all that interesting, nor are they particularly clear. And there are lots of stories about magical trees or trees that come to life. The breakthrough was when he decided to make the story not about the tree at all, but about the fairy lights we put on the tree, and the fairies we put on the top.

Lots of even bigger changes have happened for Christopher this year. He's not a lawyer anymore at all! Now he works as a writer full-time, writing articles and websites for businesses, stories for children and novels for adults. He realized that he's happiest when he's using his imagination, telling stories and being creative.

Christopher has enjoyed working with the always-reliable Emily on the fourth book in the series and can't wait to collaborate with her again on the next book.

The First Christmas will be released in 2015, and will be the last book in the series!

ABOUT THE ILLUSTRATOR

Devastated when she didn't receive her Hogwarts letter, Emily decided to do something just as magical so decided to illustrate and write children's books instead! She has worked on a number of other children's books, both writing her own stories and illustrating for other authors. More of her work can be seen at www.emilyharperillustration.co.uk.

As well as her illustration work, Emily works as an animator, workshop leader and supply teacher so she gets to spend lots of time with the most imaginative people there are - children!

As always, Emily has enjoyed bringing Christopher's creations to life, particularly the flying pigs!